THE
S

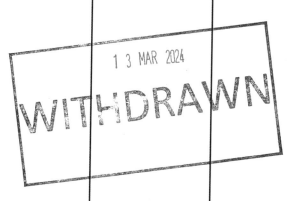

PAMELA
BUTCHART

Look out for:

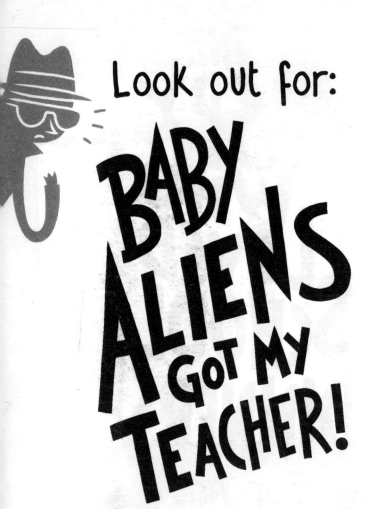

BABY ALIENS GOT MY TEACHER!

For Andy,
on our
wedding day.

First published in the UK in 2014 by Nosy Crow Ltd
The Crow's Nest, 10a Lant Street
London, SE1 1QR, UK

Nosy Crow and associated logos are trademarks and/or registered
trademarks of Nosy Crow Ltd

Text copyright © Pamela Butchart, 2014
Cover and illustrations copyright © Thomas Flintham, 2014

The right of Pamela Butchart and Thomas Flintham to be identified
as the author and illustrator respectively of this work has been asserted
by them in accordance with the Copyright, Designs
and Patents Act 1988.

A CIP catalogue record for this book will be available from the British Library.

Printed and bound in the UK by Clays Ltd, St. Ives Plc

Papers used by Nosy Crow are made from wood grown in
sustainable forests.

ISBN: 978 0 85763 257 9

www.nosycrow.com

Contents

Even Dad Can't Save Me This Time!

Sometimes when my mum is telling me off, my dad says, "Ah, leave her be. Her heart's in the right place. Isn't it, Izzy?"

And I say, "I hope so!" Because if it's not, it could be ANYWHERE! Like in my arm or my knee or even my big toe! And THAT

1

is a bit worrying. Especially if the doctors need to find it to make sure I'm not dead or something.

Dad usually says things like that when he's sticking up for me because I've done something that makes Mum go MAD. Like the time I told Mum to close her eyes and made her kiss the daddy-long-legs that lost two of its legs when I stood on them by mistake. But then Mum opened her eyes because it tickled her nose. And she screamed, and hit it away. And that made the daddy-long-legs lose ANOTHER leg.

I tried to tell Mum I was only trying to get

her to kiss it better, like she used to do to my leg when I was little. But Mum just kept screaming. And then Dad told me to put the daddy-long-legs outside, and I started crying because I didn't think Martin would survive outside without all his legs.

Another time Mum went mad was the time Dad wasn't well, so I made him a cup of warm milk. But then Dad said that the milk looked a bit green, and that it tasted funny, but I told him to drink it anyway for the NUTRIENTS.

And then Mum shouted, "Izzy! Down here, PLEASE!" And then she said that it was NOT OK to put milk in the kettle, and that

it was DEFINITELY not OK to put broccoli in too. And then she said that was why the kettle had smoke coming out of it, and also why I was now banned from the kitchen for life.

But there was one time that not even Dad could save me from getting into DEEP TROUBLE. And that was the time that had to do with the spy who loved school dinners, and France, and the *Discovery* ship and all the ice-cream and scurvy (which is a deadly skin disease). So it was VERY SERIOUS! And Jodi (that's my friend) says that we are all lucky to be alive!

The New Girl

It all started when Miss Jones (that's our teacher) told us that a new pupil would be joining our class, and that she was French, and that she was from France, and that her name was Mathilde (which sounds a bit like Matilda, but isn't).

We all got REALLY excited about the new girl coming. And it was even better because she was coming all the way from another country!

Miss Jones made us do lots of French lessons before Mathilde arrived, and then she gave us all French dictionaries so we could look up all the words Mathilde said, and find out what they meant.

Miss Jones said that Mathilde was very good at speaking English, and that she knew lots of English words. But she also said that we should try to use French words, so that we could make Mathilde feel more at home,

and also to practise our French.

I was really pleased when Miss Jones said that Mathilde knew lots of English words, because I am not very good at French, and I wanted to be able to speak to the new French girl and ask her if she lived beside Disneyland Paris. And if she had ever eaten frogs' legs or snails, like Dad said she might have.

Mum got annoyed at Dad when he told me about the snails and the frogs' legs. She said, "Don't be daft, Stewart!" (That's my dad.) "Just because someone's French doesn't mean they eat frogs' legs!"

And then she said, "That's like saying that just because YOU'RE from Scotland YOU eat haggis and wear a kilt all day!"

8

And then Dad burst out laughing and said, "I've never eaten haggis in my LIFE! And I HATE my kilt!"

And then Mum said, "Exactly!" and threw a tartan sock at Dad and walked away.

Then Dad said that Mum was right, and that Mathilde probably DIDN'T eat frogs' legs OR snails. And that he had only been joking, and that it wasn't really a funny joke. But I decided that I was going to ask Mathilde about the snails anyway, just to be sure. Because we get LOADS of snails in our garden and I could collect them all in a box and give them to her, because I don't really like the snails, and I definitely wouldn't eat any of them.

So anyway, on Friday Miss Jones asked me to stay in at break to talk about Mathilde coming. Miss Jones said that she wanted me to take SPECIAL CARE of Mathilde when she got here and make sure she settled in OK. So I said that I would, and I was REALLY excited because EVERYONE wanted to be friends with the new French girl, and I couldn't WAIT to tell Zach and Jodi and Maisie that I had been the one picked to be in charge of her.

Zach and Jodi and Maisie are my friends.

Zach lives in the flat downstairs from us, and Mum says we have been friends since we were babies. And I have been friends with Jodi since the first day of primary school when Jodi wouldn't let go of her mum's leg until me and Zach pulled her fingers away one at a time.

And Maisie is our new friend. We weren't really friends with her until two months and one week ago, when we all went through a TRAUMATIC EXPERIENCE together when we thought Miss Jones was an alien.

I used to think that Maisie was a bit weird, because she's always fainting and stuff, and also because she's a bit of a scaredy-cat. But now I think she's great.

So anyway, I told everyone about how I was in charge of looking after Mathilde. And Zach said that we could take Mathilde to The Den. But then Jodi said she wasn't sure in case Mathilde told.

The Den is the secret room that nobody except for us knows about under the stairs that lead to the toilets. And it's where we have our secret meetings and stuff. The Den has loads of cool things in it like chalk from the old days, and a sink, and even a kettle! We think it's where the old caretaker used to have his breakfast and hide from the Head Teacher because he didn't like him. But now the old caretaker has retired and we've got the key. But we don't bother locking the door any more because nobody except for us knows that The Den exists, and also because we lost the key.

So anyway, I said to Jodi that we would HAVE to show Mathilde The Den, because Mathilde had to stay with me AT ALL

TIMES. And then I said that I HAD to come to The Den to do important things, like feeding the moth, and making plans for the swimming pool we were digging behind the bike shed, and that Mathilde would have to come too. And Jodi couldn't really argue with that, so she just said OK.

So we made a "WELCOME MATHILDE!" poster and put it up on the wall.

And then we tidied up a bit. And then we wiped all the dust off a bucket so that Mathilde would have a chair to sit on. And then we went back to class.

Hello, Yes, Leg!

On Monday Miss Jones said that Mr Murphy (that's the Head Teacher) would be bringing Mathilde to our class at 10 a.m. And that I would sit with her, and that I would be in charge of loads of stuff like speaking to her, and taking her for lunch, and taking her to the toilet. Miss Jones said that I was also in charge of telling Mathilde all about our Antarctica project and about how we were learning about all the animals that live in Antarctica, and about the Antarctica explorers, and about how the weather in Antarctica is so SEVERE that you would probably die instantly if one of your gloves fell off by mistake.

I was really excited to be the one picked to be in charge of Mathilde, and I was WELL PREPARED because I had made Dad take me to Asda so I could get an extra pencil case, extra pencils and a new glitter pen, so that I could share with Mathilde if she didn't have any new school stuff yet.

And I had polished my good school shoes, and Mum had even ironed my socks so that I could look PROFESSIONAL. Because, like Maisie said, I was practically a teacher now.

Then before I went to bed I had drawn a picture of what I thought Mathilde would look like, and I gave her dark hair, and blue eyes, and a green

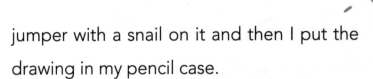

jumper with a snail on it and then I put the drawing in my pencil case.

So anyway, I kept looking at the clock to see if it was 10 a.m. yet, and I think the clock must have been needing new batteries or something because it was taking AGES to get to 10 o'clock, and I was just about to ask Miss Jones if she could fix it when Mr Murphy appeared at the door with a REALLY tall girl.

I didn't realise that it was Mathilde at first, because the girl was so tall I thought maybe she was one of the prefects or something.

But then Mr Murphy said, "Good morning,

4J! This is Mathilde." And I was SHOCKED! Because Mathilde was really tall, and she had short blonde hair, and she didn't look ANYTHING like the picture I had drawn.

And then everyone said, "W-E-L-CO-M-E, M-A-T-H-I-L-D-E," really slowly, like Miss Jones had made us practise so that we said Mathilde's name right.

Miss Jones shook Mathilde's hand, and then she waved at me to come up to the front. But then Mr Murphy looked at me funny. And then he said something to Miss Jones. But Miss Jones just smiled and told me to introduce myself.

But I had forgotten how to introduce myself in French, so I just said, "Hi. I'm Izzy," and shook her hand like Miss Jones had done, because I didn't really know what else to do.

Then Mr Murphy looked at me funny again, so I just smiled at him like Miss Jones had (even though I am not actually speaking to the Head Teacher at the moment, but I will tell you all about that later).

Then when Mr Murphy went away, Miss Jones starting doing the lesson REALLY slowly so that Mathilde would understand. And sometimes she tried to use the French words. And sometimes she forgot what they were, and then she had to use the French dictionary.

But I couldn't really pay attention to what Miss Jones was saying to us because I was still thinking about how TALL Mathilde was, and how SHORT her hair was, and how she didn't look anything like I'd thought she would!

And then I looked at Mathilde's hands and saw that she had long fingernails with purple nail varnish on them. And we are NOT ALLOWED nail varnish in our school. Not since we were making the cakes for the school cake sale and Jodi had borrowed her mum's fake nails and stuck them on with Pritt Stick, and then one of them had fallen off in the cake mix, but Jodi didn't know, so she just kept stirring and making the cakes. But then Lynsey Perry's mum found a blue fingernail in her lemon sponge and said that she could have "CHOKED TO DEATH!"

So that's when nail varnish, and nails, and

cake sales got banned from our school, and we all got a letter home about it. And now Mum clips my nails every Sunday night, and sometimes she does our cat's too, and she even uses the same clippers, which I don't think is very HYGIENIC and is probably the reason I got tonsillitis.

So I got out my new glitter pen and wrote a list in the back of my notebook. And it said:

THINGS TO TELL MATHILDE

1. We are not allowed nails, or nail varnish, or cakes.

And then I saw that Mathilde had tan tights on, and we are not allowed tan tights! We are only allowed black, or grey, or red, or white, and sometimes bare legs (but only if it's summer), but NEVER tan tights (but I don't really know why). So I added that to the list too. And then I tried to pay attention to what Miss Jones was saying.

At break time I said to Mathilde, "Do you want to see The Den?" But Mathilde didn't say anything back. So I just took her.

When we got there, Jodi and Zach and Maisie were already there. And Zach had

pretended to put the kettle on and said that he was going to make us all a cup of tea.

Zach likes making the tea even though we're not allowed to boil the kettle and there are only three cups now because Zach broke one. But none of us really likes tea anyway, so we usually just hold the cups and pretend we do.

So we gave Mathilde a cup of cold tea, but she just stared at it and didn't say anything.

So I said, "Mathilde, do you like The Den?" And we all looked at her to see what she would say. But she didn't say anything.

And then Jodi said, "ARE – YOU – OK?"

And she said it really slowly and REALLY loud. But Mathilde still didn't say anything.

Then Maisie said that maybe we needed to use the French words. But none of us could really remember any French words, except for "bonjour", which means "hello", and "oui", which means "yes", and "jambe", which means leg. So we said all of those words, but that just made Mathilde stare at us even more!

And then Maisie said that Mathilde looked a bit scared. So Zach said that we should just point to the banner that we made for her, and smile a lot. So we did. But then Mathilde looked even MORE scared. So we stopped smiling and took her back to Miss Jones.

I explained to Miss Jones about how there was something wrong with Mathilde, because she wouldn't speak any English words, and not even any French words.

And then we watched while Miss Jones tried to get Mathilde to speak. But she wouldn't. Not even when Miss Jones said a full sentence to her in French. Mathilde just stared at her like she had stared at us.

Miss Jones told Mathilde that it was OK if she didn't want to speak right now. And then she told us that Mathilde was probably just

shy and that we should be patient with her.

But, like Mum says, I find it very hard to be patient. Like the time Mum made the Winnie the Pooh chocolate lollies for the cake sale, before cakes got banned. And I COULDN'T WAIT for them to set and go hard, so I could have one. So I kept taking them out of the fridge and drinking a bit out of the mould. And then when Mum went to get them in the morning, none of the Winnie the Poohs had any legs, and Eeyore didn't have a head.

And then Mum said, "You might as well just eat them now. I doubt anyone will pay

for these poor souls!" So I did, but they didn't taste as good as when you could drink them.

So anyway, I made sure I was PATIENT with Mathilde. And so I only asked her twice about Disneyland Paris, and the frogs' legs, and the snails. And then when she didn't answer I asked her only two more times. But she STILL didn't answer.

So I gave up. Because I was starting to think that maybe Miss Jones had got it wrong, and that maybe Mathilde COULDN'T speak any

English words. And that maybe she couldn't even speak any French words either. Or that maybe she was the wrong Mathilde, and there was another Mathilde, who was shorter, and who had dark hair and blue eyes, who had been taken to the wrong school by mistake. And I was just about to explain all of this to Miss Jones when the bell went and it was time for lunch.

Mathilde Hates Us

I couldn't **BELIEVE** what happened when we took Mathilde to get lunch. We had just sat down at the table, and I had made sure that Mathilde had everything she needed, like a knife and fork, and the Good Juice, and a milkshake. But then when we started eating, Mathilde picked up her tray and walked away!

So I shouted, "Mathilde! Where are you going? DO YOU NEED UN WEE?!" But Mathilde just ignored me and kept on walking. And then she sat down at a table at the other end of the hall, all on her own, and started eating her lunch!

I thought that Mathilde was going to get into trouble from Mrs Kidd (the evil dinner monitor) because usually you are not allowed to move seats during lunch. And Mrs Kidd makes you sit in the same seat until you are COMPLETELY finished. And she says things like, "This is NOT a buffet. Sit down!" and "DOES THIS LOOK LIKE A TAKEAWAY!" And so I knew that this was something I would have to add to the "List of Things to Tell Mathilde".

Then Zach said, "What's she doing?" And I said that I didn't know.

And that's when Jodi said, "I think she hates us."

And I got really upset, because I didn't understand why Mathilde hated us and didn't want to sit with us, or why she didn't want to answer any of my questions, or why she wouldn't even say ONE WORD to me. And then when I looked again I saw that she was writing something in her little black book.

Then after lunch when we went to class, I saw that Mathilde was already there. And that she was sitting at the wrong table.

So I told Miss Jones. And then I told her about what had happened at lunch, and about how I didn't do ANYTHING AT ALL to upset her, and that all I did was eat my lunch and ask Mathilde about snails one more time only.

Then Miss Jones said, "It's OK. If Mathilde wants to be on her own, then that's fine."

So I just went and sat down. And didn't even LOOK at Mathilde. Because if Mathilde didn't want to be friends with me, then I didn't want to be friends with her.

L'Cola

On Tuesday, Miss Jones said that we had to make an information poster about our favourite Antarctic animal.

To begin with I was going to do it about penguins, but then I didn't want to any more because it reminded me about the argument

I'd had with my Uncle Lou from London at the weekend (who can be **VERY** annoying even when he's being nice and bringing me gifts).

Me and Uncle Lou had had a bit of an argument because he got me a pencil case with polar bears on it and said it was because I was doing my project on Antarctica. So I said that I liked the pencil case, especially because one of the polar bears looked a bit like Zach, but that it wasn't really about my project because polar bears don't live in Antarctica. And that's when Uncle Lou started laughing at me. And then he said,

"Of course they do." And I said that they didn't. And then Mum said that it didn't really matter right now. And I said that it did because Uncle Lou was wrong about the polar bears.

And that's when Uncle Lou said that I was **"SILLY"** (which made me really annoyed). And then he said that Antarctica was the coldest place on earth and that that was where polar bears and penguins lived. So I said that he was right about the cold and about the penguins but that he was wrong about the polar bears. But Uncle Lou **STILL** didn't believe me! Even when I explained about how it was IMPOSSIBLE and that penguins and polar bears live as far away from each other as you can get, even further than Uncle Lou lives from us! And that's when Mum said that I should go and put the kettle on and that she'd make us all some tea. So I reminded her about how I was banned from the kitchen for LIFE and that's when Uncle Lou said he was going to show me on the computer about how he was right about the polar bears and about how I was wrong. So Uncle Lou searched on the computer, and that's when he found out that he was wrong and I was right. But I still said thank you for the pencil case.

So anyway, Maisie decided to do her poster on the humpback whale because she thinks they're cute, and because the humpback whale leaves Antarctica in the coldest months, and Maisie says that that's what she would do if she had to live in Antarctica because Maisie is scared of the cold and usually wears two coats to school.

But Jodi wouldn't tell us which animal she was going to do her poster on, and she kept trying to hide her poster with her hand, because she's like that sometimes. But then she said that she needed ALL of the black felt-tip pens, and so that's how we found out she was doing her poster on the EMPEROR PENGUIN, because penguins are only black and white, and you don't get white pens.

I said that I wanted to do my poster on KRILL, because it sounds funny, and Zach said that he wanted to do his poster on the SEA SPIDER (which was my second favourite, so it annoyed me a little bit when

Zach picked it). So Miss Jones said that me and Zach should work as a pair and do a really big information poster about all the different Antarctica SEA CRUSTACEANS, which are all the weird things in the sea that are not really fish, like crabs, and shrimps, and krill, and other things.

And then when we were doing our posters Zach got up and went to sharpen his pencil (even though his pencil didn't need sharpening, and he was just saying that it did so he could have a wander and look at everyone's posters). Then when Zach was finished pretending to sharpen his pencil he came back the long way, and he walked past Mathilde's table, and I saw him peeking over Mathilde's shoulder at the little black book she's always writing in. And then he looked SHOCKED.

And when he sat back down he wouldn't tell me what he'd seen. He just said, **"SSHHH!"** and grabbed my pen, and his hand was all sweaty so I knew that what he had seen was going to be serious, and also probably life-threatening.

And then Zach wrote down what he had seen in Mathilde's book. And it said:

And even though it was in French, and I'm not very good at French, I knew that the words meant

SECRET PLAN.

But then Jodi said that the French words Zach had written down could mean something completely different in English, like "SERPENT" or "RABIES". So she took charge of the French dictionary and looked up the words. And they did mean SECRET PLAN.

So then I pointed out that I was right and

Jodi was wrong, and she got annoyed. And then she said that maybe I should just guess the rest of the words myself since I was obviously OBSESSED with French.

And so I said, "FINE. I WILL!" And then she said she didn't care about the stupid French words any more and went back to her seat.

But we couldn't find "L'COLA" anywhere in the dictionary, so we didn't know what Mathilde's secret plan was about.

Then Jodi came back over, and she had OBVIOUSLY been listening, and she said, "I think we should ask Miss Jones."

But then Maisie said, "I think 'l'cola' means cola. Like the cola you drink. It probably just has an 'L' first because it's French."

But I didn't really think that Mathilde was doing a plan about cola, because I couldn't see any cola, and because we'd never seen Mathilde drinking any, and also because it didn't really make sense.

So we asked Miss Jones what **"L'COLA"** meant. And Miss Jones got really excited because she thought Mathilde had spoken to us and that was how we'd heard the word. But I told Miss Jones that Mathilde still hadn't said one word to us. And then I said that I

thought I'd heard Mathilde say **"CHEESE"** earlier, but that she was just sneezing.

So anyway, Miss Jones looked at the word and then she said it meant "cola". But we said that we didn't think it DID mean "cola", and we asked her if there was anything else it could be.

So Miss Jones looked at the word again and then she said, "Are you sure you've spelled it correctly?"

So we all looked at Zach and he said, "Yes, I'm sure." But I wasn't so sure because I think Zach might need glasses, because sometimes his eyes can read things wrong.

Like the time Mum took us to the cinema and I went to the toilet before the film and when I came out of the toilet to wash my hands Zach was standing at the sink next to me washing HIS hands. And we both screamed a little bit when we saw each other and I shouted, "You're in the GIRLS' TOILETS!"

And he said, "No, I'm NOT! You're in the BOYS' TOILETS!" And then two ladies walked in and stared at him and that's when he realised he WAS in the girls' toilets, and that he must have read the sign wrong. So he ran out as fast as he could, and he almost fell over, and I couldn't stop laughing all the

way through the film.

So anyway, I said to Miss Jones that it **MIGHT** be spelled wrong and then she said,

"OK, hold on," and she started looking on her computer.

Miss Jones is very good on her computer. And she always finds the answers to all our questions really quickly when we have questions like, "What is the hairiest animal alive?" and "Where did the first hamster come from?" and "In Turkey, how many ACTUAL turkeys are there?"

And then Miss Jones said, "Ah-HA!" and she wrote down a French word on the bit of paper and asked Zach if THIS was the word he meant to write.

And Zach looked at the word and said,

"Oh. Yes." And the word was:

L'ECOLE

Then Miss Jones told us that the word meant "SCHOOL". And then she reminded us to get on with our posters, so we did. But first we wrote out the new translation, which said:

PLAN SCHOOL SECRET.

And Jodi said, "She's got a secret plan about OUR school! That's why she's here!"

And that's when we all knew that this was going to get SERIOUS.

And then Maisie said, "Please don't let it be aliens. Please, please, PLEASE!" Because Maisie still has nightmares about aliens, even when she's awake.

But I said that I didn't think it was about aliens, and that I thought it was about SPIES instead, because spies have notebooks, and secret plans, and are probably always French.

And then I took a deep breath and said, "I think the new girl is a SPY!"

School Spy

After lunch we decided to watch Mathilde carefully one hundred per cent of the time. Because, like Jodi said, if Mathilde really **WAS** a spy and she was spying on our school then we needed to find out why. Because it was **OUR** school so it was up to us.

So Jodi said we needed to do

And that meant that I had to watch Mathilde for the first ten minutes and write down everything she did, and then Jodi would do the next ten minutes, and then Maisie, and then Zach.

So I watched Mathilde while everyone else did their posters and this is what I wrote down:

1.30 p.m. Doing her poster

1.31 p.m. Doing her poster

1.32 p.m. Still doing her poster

1.33 p.m. Just looked at me!

1.34 p.m. Doing her poster again

1.35 p.m. Just looked at me AGAIN!

1.36 p.m. Still looking at me!

1.37 p.m. Just put her hand up

1.38 p.m. Just pointed at me

1.39 p.m. Miss Jones looking at me now too

1.40 p.m. Miss Jones just told me to stop

staring at Mathilde and do my work

So we had to stop doing the surveillance and think of something else instead. Zach said that maybe we could try to peek at Mathilde's book again. But I said that it would take too long to look up all the words, one by one, in the French dictionary.

And then Maisie said we needed to find out why Mathilde was spying on us URGENTLY so that we could stop her. And then she looked a bit sick. So we decided we needed to have an URGENT

MEETING to make all the plans.

We usually have our secret meetings in The Den. But Jodi said that The Den was now "COMPROMISED", which meant that it was no longer safe to do secret meetings in because Mathilde knew where it was.

Jodi knows lots of good words that have got to do with secret missions and the police, because Jodi's mum's old boyfriend was a policeman. But Jodi's mum's new boyfriend drives an ice-cream van, and he's Jodi's favourite now.

We all think that Jodi should be a police officer when she grows up, because she's probably better than the police at investigations and she's only eight. But when the police came to our school to do a talk and asked us who wanted to join the police, Jodi never put her hand up. Then when I asked her why she didn't, she said it was because she was going to be a Ghost Hunter.

Anyway, that's when Maisie said, "We can have the meeting at my house if you want?" And we were all a bit shocked because we'd never been to Maisie's house before. So we said yes and that made Maisie really happy, and I was really excited.

Maisie's Mansion

Jodi's mum drove us all to Maisie's house after we'd had our tea, because Maisie lives really far away from us. And she has to get up earlier than we do in the morning, because it takes her longer to get to school, and she can't just walk like me and Zach do.

So anyway, I got really excited when we got to Maisie's because Jodi's mum said, "Wow! Check out the MANSION!"

And I looked out of the window and saw that Maisie's house was basically a PALACE! And then we saw Maisie standing outside with her mum and she was waving at us really fast.

Then when we got out, Maisie squealed, "Come in! Come in! I'll do a tour!" And I had never seen Maisie so hyper before, and usually it's me or Jodi or Zach that gets all hyper, so it was funny to see Maisie like that.

And then Maisie's mum said, "How

wonderful!" And then Jodi's mum asked if she could come too, because looking at other people's houses is Jodi's mum's favourite thing to do. So we all went inside.

We just left Jodi's mum to look at all the boring stuff downstairs, like the kitchen and the washing machine, and we ran upstairs as fast as we could.

I couldn't believe how many rooms were upstairs. And how high the roof was! And how big the doors were! You could fit my whole house into just one tiny bit of Maisie's house!

Then Zach said, "Is this where your upstairs

neighbours live?"

And Maisie giggled and said, "No, well, my gran used to. But then she died."

And then she looked a bit sad. And I felt bad because I didn't even know that Maisie had a gran, or that she had died.

Then Maisie said, "Come on!" and ran down to the end of the hall, which was really far away. And then she said, "This is my room," and she opened the door. And we couldn't believe it. Maisie had

THE BIGGEST ROOM IN THE WORLD!

Maisie had a huge bed with curtains around it, and a big fluffy couch, and loads of cool beanbag chairs. And there were loads and loads of books everywhere!

And then Zach said, "STAIRS!" and I turned around and saw there was a little staircase that went up to another floor. MAISIE HAD HER OWN LITTLE STAIRS!

So we ran up the little stairs, and Maisie giggled and ran after us. And then Maisie said that her room used to be the library, and that she would sometimes fall asleep in the library when she was reading all the books. And that her gran said that the library should be Maisie's bedroom since she loved all the books so much.

And I thought that Maisie's gran sounded really nice. And I felt sorry that she had died.

After we'd looked at everything, and asked all our questions, and fed Maisie's tiny fish, we sat at the big reading table, up the little stairs, and started the secret meeting.

Jodi said she thought we should have ALL the secret meetings at Maisie's from now on because it was great. And also because there were lots of books and encyclopaedias in case we wanted to find out something. And we all agreed. And Maisie just kept giggling.

I'd never seen Maisie giggle so much before, and that was when I realised that Maisie must really like us being at her house.

So anyway, we were just about to discuss

Mathilde being a spy when there was a knock on the bedroom door.

And a voice said, "COO-EE? Can I come in, please, my darling?"

And it was Maisie's mum and she had a little trolley like you get on the train, and it had LOADS of cakes and biscuits and cups of juice on it, and that's when I realised Maisie must have some sort of lift or escalator in her house somewhere, because I don't think Maisie's mum would have been able to get the trolley up the stairs by herself.

And then Maisie's mum said, "It's so WONDERFUL to have you all here! I can't

tell you how THRILLED I am you've come
to spend time with my little angel!"

That's what Maisie's mum always calls
Maisie. Except when she calls her "My little
darling," and sometimes "My little cherub,"

and one time "My little butterfly wings".

Maisie's mum started asking us loads of questions like, "Are you too hot?" and "Are you too cold?" and "Would you like to call your mum?" and "Do you need a blanket?" and "Is the juice too strong?" and "Would you like to use the bathroom?"

And then Jodi said yes, she would like to use the bathroom actually, and that's when I screamed!

I didn't scream because Jodi needed to go to the toilet (that would just be weird). I screamed because Maisie opened her cupboard door and I saw that it WASN'T a cupboard door, it was a bathroom door, and that Maisie had her own bathroom!

I would LOVE my own bathroom, because then I could keep the bath filled all the time, and use all the bath-bombs Zach's mum got me from the shop that Mum can't go into because the smell gives her a headache. And also because I wouldn't have to hold my nose and go to the toilet as fast as I can EVERY night after Dad comes out.

Sometimes I even have to go down to Zach's to use the toilet because Dad goes in there for AGES and then every time I knock on the door, he just says,

"GO AWAY!"
or
"I'LL BE AT LEAST ANOTHER TWENTY!"

And one time Zach's mum took AGES to answer the door because she was in bed, and I almost had an accident right there on Zach's doormat like our cat once did.

So anyway, then we all said we needed to use the bathroom. And Maisie's mum said to use the one along the hall, but we just said we'd wait because we all wanted to use Maisie's bathroom. And that made Maisie's

mum laugh, and then she said, "Would anyone like anything else, anything at all? Anything?" and we said, "No, thank you," and then Maisie's mum eventually went away.

Why
Spy?

After we'd all been to the toilet, we got back to work. And Jodi said the first thing we needed to do was find out **WHY** Mathilde would want to spy on **OUR** school. So we called it the **"WHY SPY?"** investigation.

Zach said that he knew more about spies

than Jodi, because spies were one of his favourite things. So we all said Zach should be in charge, and that made him look a bit shocked, because he's not usually put in charge.

Zach said that the first thing we had to do was to write down everything we knew about Mathilde because he said,

"YOU NEED TO KNOW YOUR ENEMY INSIDE OUT!"

So we did. And this is what it said:

SPY DETAILS
NAME: Mathilde

AGE: 8

HEIGHT: Giant

HAIR: Yes

FAVOURITE COLOUR: Don't know (probably green, because of the frogs' legs)

OTHER STUFF: She is French and comes from France.

She doesn't speak EVER.

She has been in our school for three days.

She doesn't want to be friends with us.

She's always writing in her little book.

She knows where The Den is.

Then Zach said that we had to think of all the reasons why Mathilde would want to spy on our school. And I couldn't really think of any reasons. But then I remembered about how Mathilde was always staring at us, especially when we were doing our Antarctica Animal posters and so I said, "Maybe she wants to steal our poster ideas! And take them to her old school in France and pretend they're hers!"

Just like Lynsey Perry did when I made a poster about healthy eating. My poster was UNIQUE, because I hadn't used pens, or pencils, or even paint; I had used real food.

I used mustard for yellow, mushed peas for green and salmon for orange. But then Lynsey Perry COPIED me, only she used boring food that didn't smell, like pasta, and raisins, and a Ryvita.

And then the Head Teacher came in to do the judging and said that Lynsey Perry's poster was VERY CREATIVE and gave it first place. And then he said that my poster was a HEALTH AND HYGIENE CONCERN and put it in the bin. So that's when I fell out with the Head Teacher and I'm still not really speaking to him.

So anyway, Zach said that we needed more

ideas. And Jodi said that she had loads. And they were:

IDEA 1: Mathilde wants to steal our brilliant Antarctica project and take it to her old school (which was the same as my idea).

IDEA 2: Mathilde wants to steal Miss Jones and take her to France because she's really good at doing projects.

IDEA 3: Mathilde wants to steal our whole school because her old school is probably crumbling to the ground and they need a new school. So they sent a spy to see if our school is the best.

And then Zach said that Jodi wasn't allowed to give any more ideas because HE was in charge now, and she was just trying to TAKE OVER as usual. And we all knew it was true because Jodi doesn't really like it when anyone is in charge that isn't her.

Like the time Zach's mum said we could paint Zach's room. And Zach was in charge because it was his room. So Jodi was only allowed to paint the door, and I was allowed to paint the small wall, and Maisie was just going to watch and wear Zach's Darth Vader mask because she was scared of the smell. And Zach was going to paint the rest.

But then when Zach went to the toilet, Jodi finished painting the door really fast and just started painting the big wall too! And then she said she wanted to do the ceiling, and also that she wanted to change the colour. And by the time Zach came back, Jodi had COMPLETELY TAKEN OVER!

So anyway, we still weren't sure why Mathilde was spying on us. And I didn't really think Jodi's ideas were right because none of them explained why Mathilde hadn't spoken to anyone since she got here. And it seemed a bit strange to come all the way from France just to steal our poster ideas (even though they ARE excellent and will probably be put up in a museum about Antarctica when they are finished).

But then I remembered something I'd heard Mr Murphy say at assembly last week, about a School Inspector coming to our school. And that the School Inspector would be "WATCHING US VERY CLOSELY" and "WRITING EVERYTHING DOWN". And that we were all to be "AS GOOD AS GOLD".

And then I'd heard the office ladies say that

Mr Murphy was worried in case the School Inspector didn't like our school, and that if they didn't they would **"SHUT US DOWN FOR GOOD!"** And we'd all get separated, and have to go to horrible schools.

So I told everyone about what Mr Murphy had said, and explained that Mathilde was obviously the **SCHOOL INSPECTOR**. And that was why she was spying on us. And that she was going to **SHUT DOWN** our school and we'd all get separated!

And then Maisie got really upset and said that she didn't want us to all get separated. And then we had to put her to bed and shut

the little bed-curtains for ten minutes just to calm her down. Then, when she was calm, she opened the little bed-curtains and told us to come in.

Zach said that he didn't think a French girl who was only in our year would be allowed to be a School Inspector, because a School Inspector would DEFINITELY be a grown-up. So I told everyone about the programme I watched with Dad, where the boss of a big supermarket DISGUISED herself with a wig and glasses and pretended that she wasn't the boss. And then she was able to work behind the cheese counter and find out what the people who worked for her REALLY did when she wasn't there. And what they REALLY did was say mean things about her, and eat all the cheese, and sometimes the ham, and sell the cheese that had fallen on the floor.

So I said, "Mathilde's not REALLY a new pupil from France. She's a grown-up School Inspector in DISGUISE. So she can spy on us, and find out what we're REALLY like. She's UNDERCOVER!"

And then Maisie said, "But Mathilde HATES us! She's going to SHUT US DOWN! I don't want to get separated!" And then she mumbled something about new schools, and new germs, and then she fainted. So we just tucked her in and kept on having the meeting, because there's not

much else you can do when Maisie faints.

And then I said that Mathilde probably couldn't talk because if we heard her voice we would find out that she wasn't French! And also that she was really a grown-up, because her voice would sound all old, and boring, and she wouldn't be able to help herself from saying things like "Be quiet!" and "Pick that up!" and "Stop licking your arm hairs!"

And then Zach said that made complete sense, and that he believed me. And that Mathilde must be wearing a FACE MASK.

But then Jodi said, "I still don't think she's

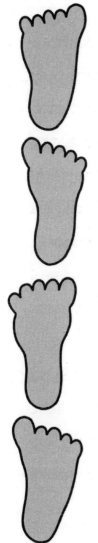

a grown-up. She's tall, but she's not GROWN-UP tall!" And Jodi had a good point, because I don't think you can really disguise yourself to be smaller than you are.

Then Maisie mumbled, "My Auntie Jean is only four feet tall." But none of us really knew how tall four feet was. So we drew around Jodi's foot on a bit of paper with a pen. And then we cut out four Jodi feet shapes, exactly the same, and lined them up to see how tall four feet was.

I was the one who said we should draw around Jodi's foot, because I know FOR A FACT that she has the biggest feet out of all of us (even though she said she didn't, and that it must be Zach, because he's a boy, and then she went into a huff after Zach put his foot against her foot and hers WAS bigger).

So anyway, we all looked at the feet ladder we'd made and Jodi said, "That's tiny! Are you sure your auntie isn't six or seven feet tall?" But Maisie said she WAS sure. Because one time when she was at the carnival with her Auntie Jean, the man who does the rollercoaster said, "You've got to be four feet one inch to go on this ride, little girl, and you're only four feet." But then the man saw that Maisie's auntie was NOT a little girl. And also that she was very angry. So he let her go on. And Maisie said that the rollercoaster made her VIOLENTLY SICK, even though she didn't go on, and she was just in charge of holding the bags.

So eventually, Jodi agreed that this meant it was DEFINITELY POSSIBLE that Mathilde was actually a grown-up School Inspector, disguised as a French girl called Mathilde, but that she was actually an UNDERCOVER SCHOOL INSPECTOR SPY.

It's All in the EYES!

After school on Wednesday we all went to see my granddad in the Home, because Mum said we could interview him for our project, because now we were learning about Antarctic explorers and about how a long time ago Captain Scott sailed all the

way to the Antarctic in a ship called the *Discovery*. And Granddad knows all about ships because he was born in the olden times, when people sailed their boats to the shops to get bread and milk instead of using a car, and before shoes were invented. But we decided we didn't want to ask Granddad about explorers and ships any more. We wanted to ask him about SPIES.

I wish I lived in the Home with Granddad, because everyone gets their own big room, and a bed that goes up and down, and the nurses bring you ice-cream and jelly every day, and next door to Granddad's room there's a magician called Mighty Marv. And Mighty Marv does his magic tricks after dinner every night in the lounge. And then he and Granddad talk about The War, and how rubbish the TV is nowadays, and sometimes potatoes. And then they both fall asleep for a bit. But then I get bored and I have to shake them really hard to wake them up so they can tell me more good stories about the potatoes.

Granddad knows LOADS about spies and secret missions, because he was very high up in The War, and he was called an Intelligent Officer. Granddad says that I have to keep everything he tells me "TOP SECRET" because he thinks Mr Thomson who sits across from him in the TV room is a spy. And that's why Granddad demanded to have a FIREPROOF TITANIUM SAFE in his room. So he could keep his medals, and inventions, and the mobile phone Mum gave him in it, in case Mr Thomson's after them.

Mum doesn't believe Granddad when he tells us about Mr Thomson and how he steals his jelly when he isn't looking, and about how he thinks Mr Thomson sneaks out of the Home every night and reports back to his commander.

Mum says Granddad sometimes says things that aren't true or that don't make sense. Like when he gives me 5p and tells me not to spend it all in the same shop.

But I always give Granddad a hug and say thank you for the 5p anyway, even though it would be quite hard not to spend it all in one shop, because not a lot of things cost less than 5p. But I visit Granddad all the time, so now I have a family-size orange squash bottle filled with 5p's!

Mum said that sometimes Granddad forgets that it's not still wartime because his brain is old. And then Mum said that my brain was young and healthy. And then I couldn't stop thinking about brains for ages. And wondering what my brain looked

like, and what colour it was. And what Granddad's brain looked like, and what colour his was. And I decided that my brain was probably yellow with bits of orange, and that Granddad's was probably grey with a tiny bit of pink in the middle, like Dad gets his steak done.

So anyway, when we got to the Home Granddad was sleeping in the TV room. So we sat quietly and pretended to watch the TV until Mum went out to speak to the nurses. And then when she was gone we shook Granddad until he woke up.

But we must have given Granddad a fright

because when he woke up he shouted,

"GET YOUR OWN TEETH!"

really loud, and Maisie squealed and hid under a chair.

But then Granddad sat up and put his finger in his mouth and felt all his teeth. And then he said, "Thank goodness! I thought old boy Thomson was off with them again!

Pulled them **RIGHT** out my mouth while I was sleeping yesterday! He's up to no good, that one."

But then Granddad saw us all standing there staring at him. And then he said, "OK. What's all this then? And what's with the serious faces?"

So I told Granddad about how we needed to find out everything about spies

And then I asked him how he knew for sure

that Mr Thomson was a spy. And that's when Granddad leaned forwards and told us to come close. So we did. And then he said, "It's all in the eyes!"

And then Granddad told me to look at Mr Thomson, so I did. And then he said, "Look. LOOK! He's staring RIGHT at me!" But when I looked, I was sure that Mr Thomson had his eyes closed, and also that he was sleeping. But when I told Granddad he said, "That's EXACTLY what he wants you to think!" So Jodi got out her pad and pen and wrote down,

"IT'S ALL IN THE EYES."

So we told Granddad all about Mathilde, and about how we thought she might be a grown-up disguised as a French girl called Mathilde. And he listened very closely to everything we said and then he said, "Hmmmmmm" for ages.

So I asked Granddad if he had ever seen a spy that was our age before, and he said,

"No, don't think so. But now that you mention it, that WOULD be a good disguise!"

So Zach said, "Do you think a spy that was really old, like you, could make themselves look young, like us?"

And Granddad said, "Definitely. Those spies can do anything."

And then Granddad stared at each one of us, and his eyes went really small, and then he said, "I wouldn't be surprised if SHE was an old spy girl herself!" and he pointed at Jodi.

So Jodi explained how she wasn't a spy, actually, and that she was just taking all the notes to make sure we didn't forget everything. And that it was hard because I was talking too fast. And then Granddad said, "And that's EXACTLY what a spy would say!"

So we told Granddad about Mathilde's little black book. And about how she was always watching everybody. And about how she was always writing everything down. And about the

"PLAN SCHOOL SECRET."

And about how she had never even spoken one word to anyone, even though Miss Jones said she could. And then Granddad said, "Good grief, girl! That DOES sound like you've got a spy on your hands!" And that's when we knew we were in serious trouble.

Then Granddad said, "You'd better be on your guard. Stay one step ahead of her at all times."

And Jodi said, "Don't worry. We'll stay at least four feet away from her at all times. We've got a feet ladder."

And then Granddad said, "Spies in the school, eh? What are they up to, eh?"

So we told Granddad all about how Mr Murphy had said that there was a School Inspector coming. And that it was very serious. And that the School Inspector would be taking lots of notes. And about how I'd heard the office ladies saying that the School Inspector was going to be watching us, and that if they didn't like us they were going to shut our school down for good. And how we'd all get separated and have to go to horrible schools. But then Granddad didn't say anything back. And then I saw that he had fallen asleep.

So Zach said, "What now?"

And Jodi said, "We're on our own. It's up to us."

And I knew that she was right. And I knew we had to do something to stop Mathilde. And that we had to do it FAST. So we pulled Maisie out from under the chair and ran to find Mum.

The Shepherd's Pie Spy

On Thursday, Jodi said that she had come up with a "BRILLIANT PLAN". And that she had been "UP ALL NIGHT" reading about spies on the Internet after her mum had gone to sleep. Jodi's not allowed to use the computer when she's supposed to be sleeping. And she's not even allowed to use the computer without checking with her mum first, ever since the time she ordered ten pizzas by mistake, instead of just one like her mum had asked her to do. And then when the pizza man delivered the ten pizzas he said, **"NO REFUNDS."** And so Jodi had to bring two of the pizzas up to my house, and she took two to Zach's house too. And then Jodi had to bring a slice of pizza to school for her lunch every day for a week.

So anyway, Jodi said she had found out lots of

"VITAL INFORMATION!"

And then she said that if you're a spy, and you get found out, then you're not allowed to be a spy any more. Because everyone knows who you really are.

Jodi said that if we could PROVE to Miss Jones, and Mr Murphy, and everybody else

that Mathilde **WAS** a grown-up Undercover School Inspector Spy, then her **"COVER WOULD BE BLOWN!"** And she'd have to go and be a spy somewhere else. And our school would be safe.

So we all said it was a brilliant plan, because it was. But Jodi said that she hadn't actually finished the plan yet. And that this was just **STAGE 1**. And that **STAGE 2** was actually coming up with a way to prove that Mathilde was a grown-up disguised as a pupil.

And then Maisie said, "I think I've got an idea." And we all listened closely, because Maisie speaks really quietly, and also because she was whispering because we're not supposed to be talking and making plans when we are doing our numeracy.

And then Maisie said, "I can smell shepherd's pie!" And then she told us her plan.

We all thought the Shepherd's Pie Plan was a great plan! And I said we were very lucky that Maisie has such a good sense of smell and that she was able to smell that the dinner ladies were cooking shepherd's pie all the way from the classroom.

Maisie says that she's so scared of shepherd's pie that she would probably be able to smell it even if it was a hundred miles away. And I believe her, because one time when we were all making a giant cardboard spider at my house, Maisie started screaming and said she could smell fire! So we dialled

999 right away and asked for the fire brigade. And then when they got there Mum went mad and shouted,

"WHAT FIRE? WHAT FIRE?!"

And it turned out that there was NOT a fire in our house. But downstairs Zach's mum HAD lit a smelly candle in her bathroom because she'd had an upset stomach. So Maisie is very good that way.

So anyway, the plan was to watch Mathilde VERY CLOSELY at lunchtime and see how she REACTED to the shepherd's pie. All the pupils at our school HATE the shepherd's pie, so we knew that if Mathilde really WAS just a pupil like us, then she would hate it too. Especially since the dinner ladies always give you too much and then moany Mrs Kidd (the evil dinner monitor) makes you eat it all.

Mrs Kidd always makes us eat stuff we don't want to. And she's ALWAYS moaning at us. Things like: "Take your coat off! Or you won't get the benefit when you go outside!" (which doesn't make sense). Or: "Izzy, were you born in a barn?" And to begin with I just said, "I don't know," because I wasn't sure.

But then I checked with Mum and I wasn't.

So anyway, for some strange unknown reason, all the teachers seem to LOVE the shepherd's pie at our school. And they love it so much that they take it back up to their classrooms so they can eat it on their own, like I sometimes do when Mum gets me my favourite chocolate fudge from the expensive shop.

So, the Shepherd's Pie Plan was to watch Mathilde to see what she did with her shepherd's pie (like a test). And if she LIKED the shepherd's pie then that would be STRONG EVIDENCE that she was a grown-up spy. And it would also be disgusting.

We all hate the shepherd's pie so much that we try EVERYTHING not to eat it. Zach squashes his together so it looks smaller, and then he asks Mrs Kidd if he can go because he only has a small bit left. And Jodi usually just eats it really fast and holds her nose and drinks loads of juice at the same time so she doesn't taste it as much.

But Maisie gets really dizzy when it's shepherd's pie day, because Maisie gets really dizzy a lot when she's scared about things like shepherd's pie, or yellow pens, or Pancake Day. So Mrs Kidd doesn't make Maisie eat the shepherd's pie any more, after the time Maisie fainted head first into her plate and splattered shepherd's pie all over Mrs Kidd's blouse.

One time I pretended that I was going to faint when we were walking in line to the dining hall, because I smelled the shepherd's pie. But Mrs Kidd just told me to keep walking and then she said, "You should have won an Oscar for that performance, young lady!" and then she made me eat it anyway.

I even used to bring a packed lunch every Wednesday, so that I didn't have to eat it. But then the dinner ladies kept changing the day, and I'm sure Mrs Kidd was the one who told them to do that on purpose so I would have to eat it.

So now I don't bother bringing a packed

lunch. And I just take AGES to eat mine, because shepherd's pie is my most disgusting food to eat. And I know Mrs Kidd probably watches me the WHOLE TIME, so I can't even drop some on the ground, or put it on Zach's plate when he's not looking.

So when Mathilde took her tray up to get her dinner, we watched her VERY CAREFULLY. And that's when she failed the first shepherd's pie test. Because when the dinner lady asked her if she wanted one ice-cream scoop of shepherd's pie or two, Mathilde held up TWO FINGERS! And we couldn't believe our eyes!

So I said, "She **MUST** be a grown-up! There's **NO WAY** a normal human pupil would ask for two scoops!" And I was just about to write **"FAIL"** down on our **"EVIDENCE CHART"** that Jodi had made

when Maisie said, "Maybe she doesn't know what shepherd's pie is!" And I thought that probably made sense, because I don't think they have shepherd's pie in France, and when I went to Disneyland two summers ago I didn't see any there.

So Zach told us to put "PASS" next to the first test. But then Jodi said it would be better if we just put a question mark instead, because we weren't sure. So that's what we did. And then we moved on to Shepherd's Pie Test 2.

Test 2 was to watch Mathilde's face and see what happened when she ate the shepherd's pie. And to find out if she tried to hide it, or drop it on the floor, or put it in her bag, like everyone else did.

So we sat down and watched her. And that's when we COULDN'T BELIEVE OUR EYES AGAIN! And Jodi make a sick sound, and Zach said, "What's WRONG with her?!" And Maisie said, "What? What's HAPPENING?" because she couldn't see, because she's too small, and also because she had her eyes closed.

So I said, "She FINISHED IT... and she's going up for SECONDS!"

Top Stinking Secret

For the first time in our lives, we ate ALL of our shepherd's pie, just so Mrs Kidd would let us leave the table quickly. Then we all ran back to the classroom to find Miss Jones.

We told Miss Jones all about Mathilde. About how she wasn't even French. And

about her face mask. And about how she was an Undercover School Inspector Spy. And that she was probably a hundred years old or something.

But Miss Jones just STARED at us and didn't say anything. And I thought it was because she was just as shocked as we were that our school was going to get shut down, and that she would probably have to go and teach at the Big School, which she once said she'd rather swim with sharks than do.

But then Miss Jones said that she had no idea what we were talking about, and that we were talking too fast. And then she said,

"I've asked you all just to be **PATIENT** with Mathilde."

And that's when Maisie screamed at the top of her lungs, "Miss Jones, don't you understand?! SHE'S A SHEPHERD'S PIE SPY!"

Maisie had to have a little lie-down beside Miss Jones's desk after she screamed. And I thought Miss Jones was going to need a lie-down too, because she was SHOCKED at how loud Maisie had screamed. And so were we! But at least Miss Jones was taking us seriously now because she said, "Right. You three, sit down. What's all this about shepherd's pie? And why is Maisie screaming? And who's a SPY?!"

So we explained everything. But we did it a bit slower this time, because sometimes it takes grown-ups ages to understand simple things like Undercover School Inspector Shepherd's Pie Spies. Because their brains are not as fresh as our brains, just like Granddad's brain.

And when we were finished Miss Jones said, "OK. I'm going to show you something. Something that is VERY important. Something that you can't EVER tell another living person about."

And we didn't know WHAT Miss Jones was about to show us, but we knew that it was something

And then Miss Jones said, "Do you promise not to tell **ANYONE** what I'm about to show you?" And we said yes. And Jodi took my hand and she squeezed it really tight. And then Miss Jones showed us.

The Race to Conquer the Chocolate Trifle

Miss Jones picked up the bin next to her desk and lifted the lid. And there it was. A lump of disgusting shepherd's pie.

And that's when Miss Jones told us that none of the teachers liked the shepherd's pie either! And that the only reason they always took their trays back to their classrooms was so they could put it in the bin without the dinner ladies seeing. And then Miss Jones said she was a bit scared of the dinner ladies.

Then Miss Jones said that Mathilde must just LIKE the shepherd's pie, and that that wasn't suspicious. And that it certainly didn't mean she was a grown-up or a spy.

Miss Jones said that there was

NO WAY

Mathilde was actually a grown-up School Inspector Spy, because she had actually met Mathilde's mum and dad, and she had even visited her house with Mr Murphy before Mathilde came to the school. Then she told us that she had just found out that the school inspection had been CANCELLED until next year, and that Mr Murphy was ECSTATIC and that there were definitely no Inspector Spies in the school. And then she made us promise that we would stop doing the investigation about Mathilde, so we said we would.

So we all just tried to forget about Mathilde being a spy. Because now that the school inspection was cancelled, it didn't make any sense that Mathilde would be a grown-up Undercover School Inspector Spy. But forgetting about it was a very difficult thing to do, because Mathilde STILL hadn't said a word to anyone, and she was STILL looking suspicious and writing in her little book all the time. But we'd promised Miss Jones we wouldn't do the spy investigation any more, so we couldn't really do anything about it.

But then that afternoon something happened that we just COULDN'T ignore.

It happened when we were watching a film about the Antarctic explorers. The film was great because it was all about Captain Scott and how he sailed the *Discovery* ship all the way to Antarctica over a hundred years ago when he was trying to be the first person in the world to discover Antarctica and reach the South Pole. But then just when Captain Scott got there, he found out that someone had beaten him! And that an explorer from Norway had got there first.

I felt really sorry for Captain Scott because what happened to him was EXACTLY the same as when Mum said that if I ate my broccoli I could have the last bit of chocolate trifle that was in the fridge. So I ate my broccoli as fast as I could, even the stems, but then when I got to the fridge and opened it I found that someone had already beaten me to it. The trifle was gone! But it

had not been a man from Norway who had beaten me to the trifle; it had been Dad (even though he said it wasn't when I questioned him about it. But I know that it was because he had chocolate on his chin).

So anyway, we were all watching the film, and it was dark because the curtains were closed and the lights were off. And I don't know what made me do it, because we weren't even supposed to be investigating Mathilde any more, but I looked over my shoulder to see what Mathilde was doing. And I couldn't believe it. Mathilde was **GLOWING!**

What's GLOWING On?!

I stared at Mathilde for ages. Her face was glowing! And she was staring at something on her desk.

It took my brain **AGES** to understand what was going on, but then I realised that Mathilde had some sort of torch pen!

So I nudged Maisie and told her to look. But that was a bad idea, because the second Maisie saw that Mathilde was glowing, she fainted on me. And for such a small person, it sometimes hurts when Maisie faints on you.

So anyway, I DESPERATELY needed to get Zach's and Jodi's attention so they could see that Mathilde was up to something, but I couldn't really move because Maisie was in my way. So I looked to see what Miss Jones was doing, and she was busy watching the film and hadn't noticed anything about the glowing or the fainting. So I took off one of

Maisie's shoes and threw it over to beside where Zach and Jodi were sitting, and it hit Zach on the back. But then Zach shouted, "Ow!" really loud, and that made Miss Jones press pause and put the lights on. And that's when Zach and Jodi saw that it was Maisie's shoe that had hit Zach, and also that I was pretending that Maisie hadn't fainted by putting my arm around her and putting her

head on my shoulder. So they knew that something serious was going on.

Miss Jones asked Zach what was wrong and he just kind of stared at her, because Zach is not very good at coming up with lies on the spot.

So that's when Jodi said, "Sorry, miss. I sat on Zach's hand by mistake. That's all." And Zach nodded and pretended that his hand was a bit sore. And then Miss Jones was just about to put the lights off again when she noticed that Maisie had her head on my shoulder, and also that I had covered all of Maisie's face with her hair.

"Is Maisie OK?" asked Miss Jones. So I said that Maisie was fine, and that she was just hiding until the humpback whales came on, because she was a bit scared of ships. And Miss Jones just said OK and put the film back on, because she knows that Maisie is scared of most things and there's not much you can do about that.

So once the lights were off again, Jodi and Zach looked over, and I nodded over to where Mathilde was sitting. But they just kept looking over and then looking back at me. And Jodi kept shrugging her shoulders and saying, "What?" with her mouth, but not making any sound. So I put Maisie's head on my lap and turned around. And Mathilde was just sitting there pretending to watch the film! And she wasn't even glowing any more!

Once the film was finished I managed to wake Maisie up and we all went back to our tables. Miss Jones said that we should all discuss the film in our groups for five minutes and that after that she had some BIG NEWS she wanted to share with us.

Zach said he thought that the BIG NEWS Miss Jones wanted to share with us was that she was pregnant and that she was going to be having a baby. Because he said that he saw a big share-size bag of Maltesers sticking out of her bag this morning and that now the empty packet was in the bin. And then he said that only a pregnant lady could eat that many Maltesers so quickly.

But I couldn't really think about Miss Jones having a baby just now because I was too worried about what Mathilde was up to. So that's when me and Maisie told Jodi and Zach about Mathilde glowing. And about how she had a SPY TORCH PEN.

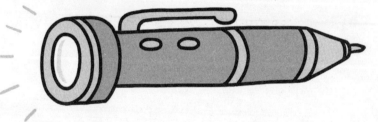

And Jodi said, "I *knew* it! So she *is* a spy, after all." And we all agreed, because Mathilde was still watching everybody all the time, and refusing to speak, and writing things down in her little book, and now she even had a SPY PEN, so she could spy in the dark!

But we had a big problem; we knew that Mathilde wasn't an Undercover School Inspector Spy because the school inspection was cancelled. But we knew that Mathilde was still a spy on some sort of secret mission. So we knew there was DEFINITELY a spy at our school, but we had NO IDEA why.

And that meant we were in

SERIOUS DANGER.

But then we couldn't talk about it any more because Miss Jones said it was time to tell us her big news. And Zach was wrong; Miss Jones's big news wasn't about babies and being pregnant, it was much better!

Miss Jones said that we couldn't visit Antarctica for our project because it was really far away and also because of the **DANGEROUS WEATHER CONDITIONS** there. And then she said that there was no way she was filling out all those "Antarctica Explorer Risk Assessment Forms". And then she had a little giggle to herself. But none of us could really see why that was funny. And then when she was finished laughing she said that because we were doing such a good job on our Antarctica project she had arranged a surprise for us. And that the surprise was that she was going to be taking us aboard the real *Discovery* ship! And as soon as she said that, Mathilde almost jumped out of her seat!

Jodi said, "Look!"

And I said, "I know!"

And Zach said, "She must love ships or something!"

And then Miss Jones started telling us all about the *Discovery*, and that someone would be showing us above deck, and below deck, and that we'd get to see where Captain Scott and his crew lived. And then she said, "And we'll get to see where they plotted their journey into the unknown!"

And then Mathilde turned and smiled RIGHT AT US!

And Maisie fainted and slipped under the desk.

Humpback Whale Marshmallowed Right at Us!

That night we HAD to break our promise to Miss Jones and start the spy investigation again. So we went to Jodi's house after our tea.

Jodi had everything ready for the meeting, and she'd already spread the duvets on the floor when we got there. And her mum had put out the really good snacks that you only get at Jodi's house on the floor. Like strawberries dipped in chocolate, and curry crisps, and mini cheeses on toasts, and the really good strawberry milkshake that only Jodi's mum can make.

Then Jodi's mum asked if she could join the secret meeting. And we felt a bit bad saying no, but we had to.

Zach said that the first thing we should do was make Miss Jones a nice card to say sorry for investigating Mathilde again after we said we wouldn't. But then Jodi said that we

didn't need to, because when we proved that Mathilde really WAS a spy and stopped her before she did whatever she was planning to do, Miss Jones would be so pleased with us that she would probably want to make US a card. And that made sense, so we all got back to the meeting.

Jodi said that the first thing we needed to discuss was "THE SMILE". But then Maisie said that she didn't really want to talk about "THE SMILE" because it was creepy, and because it had "SCARED THE LIFE OUT OF HER!"

But then Jodi said we HAD to discuss it,

because we couldn't ignore "IMPORTANT EVIDENCE". But that maybe we didn't need to actually say the word "SMILE" and that maybe we could replace "SMILE" with another word.

So Maisie said to replace "SMILE" with "MARSHMALLOW," because she loves marshmallows. And then she said to also replace the word "MATHILDE" with "HUMPBACK WHALE," because she likes them too.

But then the meeting started to get really confusing, because I said, "Humpback whale marshmallowed right at us."

And Jodi said, "That marshmallow freaked me out!"

And I said, "Do you think humpback whale marshmallowed at us because humpback whale's got a plan that has to do with ships?"

And then Zach said that he was really confused, and also that he was hungry for marshmallows now. And then he went to see if Jodi's mum had any.

Then Jodi said that she was ninety-eight per cent sure that Mathilde's secret spy mission was about the *Discovery*, and I agreed, only I was more like ninety-nine point nine per cent sure at this point because of how excited

Mathilde got when Miss Jones had said we were going aboard the ship.

Then Zach came in with loads of marshmallows and Maisie grabbed five and shoved them in her mouth to calm herself down.

And then she said, "MAFILE OA ISHON OO EELA IP ACHE USH OA URNY IOOOEEE UNOOOO!"

And we said, "What?!"

And Maisie chewed, and swallowed really fast, and then she said, "MATHILDE'S ON A MISSION TO STEAL THE SHIP AND TAKE US ON A JOURNEY INTO THE UNKNOWN!"

Attack of the Imaginary Wasp!

The next morning in class a new office lady that we'd never seen before came to the door and asked to see Mathilde.

We all watched as Mathilde stood in the doorway with the new office lady. The lady whispered something really quietly to

Mathilde, and Mathilde nodded. Then the office lady handed Mathilde a piece of paper, and Mathilde took it, looked at it, nodded again, and then put it in her cardigan pocket and went back to her seat.

As soon as Mathilde sat back down, Jodi grabbed my hand under the table and said, "Do you know what we have to do?" And I did. So I nodded. And I knew that things were about to get OUT OF CONTROL because Jodi had THAT LOOK in her eye.

I knew without even talking to Jodi about it that she wanted us to get the note out of Mathilde's pocket and read what it said. But

before I had time to guess what Jodi's plan
was, Jodi got up and walked over to Mathilde
and starting pulling at her cardigan!

"IT'S A WASP, MATHILDE! A WASP!"
she shouted. "IT FLEW RIGHT INTO
YOUR CARDI! TAKE IT OFF! TAKE
IT OFF!"

And then Jodi started shaking Mathilde's cardigan all over the place.

Mathilde looked really shocked! And then she screamed! Then Jodi looked a bit shocked. And then she said, "Oh good. It's gone now." And then she ran back over to her seat.

Miss Jones had to spend ages calming Mathilde down, and explain to her that Jodi wasn't crazy and that she had just been trying to protect her from a wasp. But I don't think Mathilde believed Miss Jones, because she kept staring over at us and giving us looks.

And then when everything had calmed

down, and we'd eventually convinced Maisie that the wasp was a hundred per cent imaginary, Jodi dropped something on our table. And it was MATHILDE'S NOTE! And this is what it said:

CAR PARK
16:00

DON'T
BE LATE

And Zach said, "Do you think she's meeting that new office lady?"

And Maisie put her hand on Zach's hand and said, "Zach. I don't think you understand." And her voice was shaking. And I just KNEW what she was about to say.

"That wasn't a new office lady. That was another spy!"

When the bell went at the end of the day, we rushed to The Den. Jodi said that we were either going to have to discuss everything in code words, or write it down instead of speaking, because now that there were two

spies in the school, The Den was probably
bugged (which meant that the spies had
put secret microphones and
cameras in it to see what we
were doing).

So we decided to write everything down in tiny writing so the cameras couldn't see it, because it was going to take too long to come up with loads of new code words.

Jodi said that she would write down what she knew about **"YOU-KNOW-WHO"** and what we were going to do about the **"YOU-KNOW-WHAT"** and then pass it around. And that we could add to it. But that we had to do it fast because we only had twenty-five minutes before **"YOU-KNOW-WHAT"**. So we did.

I was last to get the paper and by the time it reached me, this is what it said:

Humpback whale is DEFINITELY a spy

Humpback whale IS a French girl

Humpback whale has come here on a secret mission

from France to get aboard the *Discovery* and steal it!!!

Humpback whale is NOT the only spy in the school

Humpback whale has a secret spy meeting at 4 p.m. today

So there was nothing else for me to add to the note except:

WE HAVE TO GET TO THE CAR PARK NOW!

Operation Car Park

We made sure that we got to the car park early, so that Mathilde and the other spy lady she was meeting wouldn't be there yet.

Jodi made us all hide in the bushes in the car park and wait. But it was really cramped in the bushes, and itchy, and Maisie kept

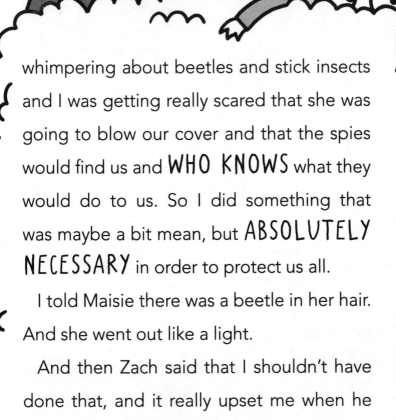

whimpering about beetles and stick insects and I was getting really scared that she was going to blow our cover and that the spies would find us and WHO KNOWS what they would do to us. So I did something that was maybe a bit mean, but ABSOLUTELY NECESSARY in order to protect us all.

I told Maisie there was a beetle in her hair. And she went out like a light.

And then Zach said that I shouldn't have done that, and it really upset me when he said that because Maisie is one of my best friends, and the only reason I made her faint was to protect us all from being captured by

French spies.

But then Zach stopped talking when Jodi said that she had a pea in her pocket, and that if Zach didn't stop talking and be quiet she would have no choice but to use it. And Zach is TERRIFIED of peas, and one time when I said that Miss Jones's baby aliens were going to look like peas, Zach fainted on the spot.

So Zach said, "No you don't."

And Jodi said, "Do you want me to prove it?"

And Zach gulped and said no.

And that's when we saw Mathilde! She came down the school steps and walked RIGHT OVER to the bushes where we were hiding! And then she stopped and looked at her watch.

And I looked at my watch, and it said: 15.59. So I knew that the other spy would be here in one minute.

And at EXACTLY four o'clock a huge limousine drove into the car park. And then it stopped and someone got out.

Me and Jodi and Zach all looked at each other in shock. It was NOT the new office lady. It was a man. The man was tall and was wearing a black suit and dark shades.

When Mathilde saw him she walked quickly towards the car and handed the man her school bag. And that's when tall shades man took her school bag, opened the door for her and let her in. And then he got back in and drove away really fast.

And then Zach let out a big breath, because he must have been holding his breath the whole time. And then he said, "She's a Spy Boss! Mathilde's a Spy Boss! She's got her own limousine and a spy chauffeur who drives her around on her missions! She's probably some sort of international boat thief!"

And we all knew he was right.

Did He Say They Ate a PENGUIN??!

The next day we all went on the bus to the *Discovery*. And I sat with Maisie at the very back of the bus, and I held her hand the whole way there, because this was a very difficult day for Maisie. Because Maisie hates buses, and ships, and we all knew that we

were going to have to do something to stop
Mathilde stealing the *Discovery* and taking
us on a

JOURNEY
INTO
THE
UNKNOWN.

Jodi and Zach sat RIGHT BEHIND
Mathilde on the bus so that they could

"WATCH HER EVERY MOVE," because that was part of the plan.

Jodi had told us all EXACTLY what to do if Mathilde tried to make a "GETAWAY" with the ship. And she had even brought the REAL police handcuffs her mum's old boyfriend had given her, in case things got "OUT OF CONTROL" and she had to do a "CITIZEN'S ARREST" (which is when a normal person becomes a police officer if they find a spy).

Before we got on the bus, Jodi had said that we were a TEAM, and that if we could deal with ALIENS then we could

DEFINITELY deal with a spy. And then she'd said that after all of our expert training we were now "READY FOR ANYTHING!" And then she'd patted us all on the shoulder and given us a Fruit Pastille each, for energy.

But I was a bit worried that I was going to forget some of the stuff we had learned at Jodi's, like the hand signals. Because there were seventeen of them, and they all meant different things like "STAY DOWN," and "GO TO THE LEFT," and "I'M GOING TO THE TOILET NOW."

So anyway, when we got off the bus at the *Discovery* I forgot all about Mathilde,

and spies, and citizen's arrests for a minute, because the ship looked BRILLIANT! And I couldn't WAIT to get on board!

But then Miss Jones came over to us with Mathilde and she said, "Izzy, Mathilde is going to join your group, OK?"

And that's when Maisie fainted again.

When we were on board the *Discovery*, the tour man told us about how the ship had been all the way to Antarctica. And then he told us all about Captain Scott. And about how he was in charge of sailing the ship. And about how cold it was in Antarctica. And about how Captain Scott and his crew had gone sledging and discovered parts of the world that no man had ever discovered before. And that that was why the ship was called the *Discovery*. We already knew all that, from doing our project, but we listened anyway. But then the tour man said something that Miss Jones HADN'T told us, and that was about how Captain Scott and the rest of the people on board had caught diseases. And about how they had all died on board the ship on their way back because of freezing to death, and hunger, and scurvy.

And then he told us all about scurvy (which is a disease that makes your skin go all scaly like a fish's, and then it all falls off, and then you die). And then Miss Jones said it was time to move on, and I think the tour man said Captain Scott ate a penguin, which is TERRIBLE! But I'm not really sure because

I couldn't really concentrate because Maisie was squeezing my hand REALLY hard, and Zach was staring at Mathilde, and Jodi wasn't really blinking, and I didn't know if it was because of the penguin thing or the JOURNEY INTO THE UNKNOWN thing.

And then I looked at Mathilde and saw that she had a MAP OF THE DISCOVERY and she was STARING at it, and not even listening to the tour man!

Then when it was time for us to explore the ship and go below deck, the man said that Group E could go first for a change, because Group A always get to go first. And then he laughed a bit. But we didn't laugh, because Group E was OUR group, and in our group there was me, Maisie, Jodi, Zach . . . and MATHILDE!

So the man showed us how to get below deck, and then he said, "Don't get lost at sea now!" And that made Maisie start shaking. And I didn't know who was going to go down the little steps first, because it looked really dark down there. And I thought that maybe Zach would do it, because we always ask him to do the things that we don't want to do, and he just does them.

But then Mathilde pushed her way to

the front and as quick as anything she disappeared down the stairs! Then Jodi started to panic and pulled out the handcuffs and shouted, **"SHE'S BELOW DECK! SHE'S BELOW DECK!"** And then she did one of her hand signals and jumped down after her. And we all went down as fast as we could!

The Ghost of Captain Scott

Below deck was a bit scary, because it was dark, and because there were people-statues, but mostly because Mathilde was NOWHERE TO BE FOUND!

So I said, "What now?"

And Jodi did the hand signal that meant

we weren't allowed to talk. And then she did the signal that meant I had to give Maisie a piggy-back in case she fainted. So I did.

Then Jodi looked at the little map and then she pointed to me and Maisie, and then to the kitchen and then to the sickbay. And we nodded. And then she pointed to all the other parts of the ship on the map, and then she pointed to Zach, and he nodded. And then she pointed to the engine room, and then to herself. And we all knew that was where Mathilde would be headed, so we nodded, because Jodi had the handcuffs.

So me and Maisie checked the kitchen. But we couldn't see Mathilde. But we did see a people-statue of an old man with a beard that Maisie thought might be Mathilde in disguise. But then we touched it, and tickled it under its arms, and it didn't move. So we

knew it wasn't real. And then when we went through to the sickbay we saw something in one of the beds. And it was a lump! But it was too dark to see what the lump was, so I said I thought it was probably just another people-statue.

But then Maisie said, "No! It's DEFINITELY the ghost of Captain Scott!" And then she started hyperventilating (which meant she started breathing really loud and really fast). And then I got really scared too because I HATE ghosts, especially ones that might have scurvy!

But then I realised that the lump might

be Mathilde, and that she might be hiding from us. So I put Maisie down and did the "MATHILDE" hand signal (which looked a bit like a bird). And then we slowly started to walk towards the lump.

And when we were close I whispered, "Is that you, Mathilde?" But the lump didn't say anything. So I reached out, and I was just about to touch the lump when it moved! And Maisie screamed! And something grabbed my shoulder! And I thought it was the ghost of Captain Scott! And that's the last thing I remember.

When I woke up I didn't really know where I was. But it was dark and it smelled funny. And then I saw three floating heads above me, and I was just about to start screaming, but then I saw that the floating heads had necks and bodies, and also that they were Jodi, Zach and Maisie. And that's when I knew I had fainted.

Then Miss Jones appeared and she looked really worried, and she said, "Izzy! Do you know where you are? IZZY?"

And then I remembered about the lump. So I said, "The lump moved. Captain Scurvy tried to get me. Somebody needs to wash my shoulder."

And that's when Miss Jones said, "OK, petal. Let's get you back on the bus for a lie-down."

And I thought that sounded like a good idea, because I felt a bit dizzy, and also because I didn't want Captain Scott and his crew of scurvy ghosts to get us.

Then when we were walking back to the bus, Jodi told me that it wasn't Captain Scott who had grabbed my shoulder, and that it had been Miss Jones. And that the lump had been Mathilde.

Jodi said that she had found Mathilde in the bed before we got there, and that she thought Mathilde had been searching for a clue, but then when she saw Mathilde wasn't moving she went to get Miss Jones.

And then I said that Jodi shouldn't have been checking OUR area, and that if she had just done her own bit then probably I wouldn't have fainted. And then Jodi said

189

sorry (and Jodi NEVER says sorry!). And I think she said it because she felt bad that I fainted, because I have never fainted before, so it was more serious than when Maisie faints.

Then when we got on the bus, we saw that Mathilde was there too. And she was lying down over the two seats at the back of the bus. And she was covering her face with her arm so we couldn't see her properly.

So I just sat quietly with Miss Jones and drank my Ribena.

Then Miss Jones told Zach and Jodi and Maisie to go back on board the ship with Mr Murphy and the rest of the class. But they said that they wanted to stay with me, so Miss Jones said OK. And then Miss Jones said how lucky I was to have such good friends. And I said yes. And then we heard that Mathilde was crying.

When we got back to school Mathilde was taken to the nurse, and we all went back to class. But we still weren't sure if Mathilde really WAS sick, or if she was just upset because her secret mission to steal the

Discovery had failed.

And then Zach said that he thought Mathilde had scurvy. And how she must have caught it from being in the sickbay bed. And then he said that he thought Mathilde had been hiding her face on the bus so we wouldn't see her scurvy skin.

And then Maisie said her arms were really itchy. And then Jodi said that HER arms were itchy. And then I noticed that my arms were itchy too, and so was my leg! And I was sure that we all had scurvy, and that we were going to die. And I was just about start crying, but then the bell went for lunch. So we forgot about having scurvy for a while because we remembered that we could go straight to The Den to have a meeting, because we all had packed lunches today.

When we got to The Den we noticed that the door was already open. And that the light was on. And I was shocked. But mostly I was scared in case Mr Murphy had found The Den, because then he would see the picture I drew of him with the tentacles that was on the wall. And I would get into DEEP TROUBLE because I had signed it with my signature and called it "Mr Murphy is Uglier than an Octopus". Which isn't a very nice thing to say, but neither is calling my poster names and putting it in the bin!

So we peeked inside to see who was in there, and it was Mathilde! And then she looked up and saw us. And that's when it happened. That's when Mathilde spoke for the very first time!

And she said, "You must help me. I am on a secret meession!"

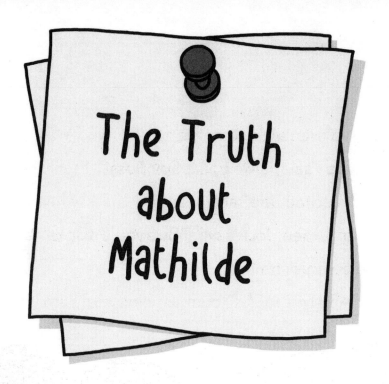

The Truth about Mathilde

None of us said anything for ages. We just stood there in SHOCK. And then we heard someone coming, and Mathilde said, "Come. Queek!" So we ran in and shut the door behind us.

Zach said, "You're talking!"

And Mathilde said, "Yes."

And I said, "Are you a Spy Boss?"

And Mathilde said, "No."

And then Jodi said, "But you ARE on a secret mission?"

And Mathilde said, "Yes." And then she started crying.

So I said, "Mathilde, you have to tell us EVERYTHING." And Mathilde nodded.

And that's when Mathilde told us that she WAS on a secret mission, and that it DID have to do with schools, but it wasn't OUR school it had to do with. It had to do with Mathilde's OLD school, back in France.

And then Mathilde cried loads. And Maisie cried a bit too, but we weren't sure why. And then Mathilde told us that she was crying because she didn't like it here, and that she missed her old school and her old friends.

And then she said that she didn't want to make new friends, and that she wanted her old friends. And then she said that was why she had ignored us.

So then I asked Mathilde why she wouldn't speak to anyone. And Mathilde said that she didn't want to speak because she wanted to go home. And that made sense.

Zach said that it sounded like Mathilde had HOMESICKNESS. And we all agreed. And I made sure Maisie understood that HOMESICKNESS isn't something you can catch.

So then Mathilde told us that her secret

mission was to ESCAPE from our school and get back to her old school in France. And that she had been making plans in her little notebook about how to get back to France since she got here. And that when Miss Jones said we were going on board the *Discovery* she had been really excited because she had finally come up with a plan that would work.

Mathilde said her plan had been to hide on board the *Discovery* until it set sail and then stay on it until it stopped in France. So Mathilde's plan wasn't very good.

And then Mathilde looked down at the ground and said, "But then you rueened it

when I was trying to hide in zee sheep."

And then Zach said that he didn't understand, and that it didn't make any sense to hide in a sheep. And also that nobody had told HIM there was a sheep on board the *Discovery*. And Maisie started whimpering because she's scared of sheep.

And Jodi said that she was a hundred per

cent sure that there weren't any sheep on board the *Discovery*, because she'd done a "FULL SWEEP," and she didn't see any sheep, or goats, or anything like that.

And then Mathilde smiled and said, "Not a sheep . . . ZEE SHEEP!"

And that's when we realised Mathilde meant ship, not sheep. And that made more sense.

And then we all said sorry to Mathilde for ruining her plan. And Mathilde listened very closely.

And then Zach said, "So, if you're not a Spy Boss, then why do you get secret messages, and have secret meetings? And why do you have a chauffeur who carries your bag, and opens the door for you, and drives you around in a huge limousine?"

And Mathilde started smiling again, and then she said, "That eez not my chauffeur! That eez my father! He drives the people around in zee limousine. That eez his new job. This is why we leave France. The message was only that my father was late to collect me and in zee rush to get back to work. This eez all."

And then she smiled a bit again, but it was a bit of a sad smile.

So I went and sat beside Mathilde, and I held her hand, and then I said, "Mathilde. We will help you with your secret meesion."

The
Paris
Plan

I knew that this was the most SERIOUS plan we had ever done. Because it was about France, and would probably involve breaking some of the rules, but mostly because Mathilde was counting on us. And I would hate it if I had to go to a new school, and I had to leave all my friends behind. So I knew that we had to do this properly.

So I got out the Big Paper. And then Jodi said, "I'll get the marker." And I knew she meant the marker pen that we stole from Miss Jones by mistake ages ago, and we'd been too scared to give it back in case she thought we stole it on purpose, so we just hid it, and we said that we wouldn't use it unless it was an ABSOLUTE EMERGENCY.

And it was. So we used it.

I said, "OK. Let's start. How are we going to get Mathilde to France?" And we came up with three ideas right away. And they were:

(1) Put her on a ship.

(2) Put her on a plane.

(3) Put her on a train.

But then Mathilde said that the ship idea should be taken off the list, because she'd already tried that and it didn't work. And also that the train one should be taken off, because trains made her feel sick.

So I said that I thought a plane would be the quickest and the best way to get Mathilde back to her old school. But then Jodi said that you needed a plane ticket to get on a plane, and we didn't have any of those. So we asked Mathilde if she still had her old ticket from when she got the plane to Edinburgh, but she said that she didn't.

Maisie said that we should just get a new plane ticket. But Mathilde said that she didn't have any Scottish money to buy a ticket, and that she only had euros. And I said that I didn't think you could use euros in the shops here.

But then I remembered about my orange squash bottle full of 5p's that Granddad had given me, and how there must have been enough in there for a hundred plane tickets to France!

So I said that we could use that, and I was getting really excited because the plan was starting to work. But then Zach said, "How will we get to the airport? It's miles away!" And he was right, because when I went to Malta with Mum and Dad we had to drive to the airport first before we even got on the plane, and it took ages. And by the time we got to the airport I had been hoping we were already in Malta.

But then I shouted, **"WAIT!"** because I realised that I had **BEEN** to France before, when we went to Disneyland in Paris (which is in France). And I remembered that we didn't get a ship **OR** a plane **OR** a train, and that we had gone in our own car!

So I told everyone about going in the car to France, and about how Dad had driven our car right on to the ferry boat. And that in the morning the boat had dropped us off in France.

But Jodi said she didn't believe me, and she said, "You're not allowed to drive cars on to boats. That would sink them."

But then Mathilde said, "Yes. Zee cars can go on zee ferry to France." And then Jodi couldn't argue any more because Mathilde is actually from France, and is French, so she knows better than Jodi.

And then Zach said that it would be easy to go in a car because his mum had a car, and so did my mum and dad. And then he said that we'd have to ask one of our mums to drive us because obviously we couldn't drive ourselves.

But Mathilde said, "NO! You cannot tell! This is a SECRET MEESSION! My parents, they cannot find out!"

And then Jodi's eyes went REALLY wide (like SCARY wide). And she started jumping up and down and saying,

"I KNOW,
I KNOW,
I'VE GOT IT,
I'VE GOT IT!"

And then she grabbed the marker right out of my hand and drew a big ice-cream van.

Choc Ices Away!

I thought Jodi's plan was BRILLIANT! It was probably the best plan that ANYONE had ever come up with. Even better than Captain Scott's plan to go sledging in all that snow in Antarctica!

The plan was that we would write a fake

order for a hundred ice-cream cones (with Flakes) to be delivered to the Eiffel Tower. And then we'd put the order in Jodi's mum's boyfriend's ice-cream van. And we'd put the orange squash bottle full of 5p's there too, to pay for it.

So then when Jodi's mum's boyfriend saw the order, he'd have to drive to Paris right away, because we'd already paid. And Mathilde would be hiding in the back, and then she'd get back her old school and her old friends in France! Jodi was a GENIUS!

So after school we all went to Jodi's house for tea. And Jodi's mum was REALLY

excited to have Mathilde over, and she kept talking to Mathilde in French, and then she would ask Mathilde if what she said sounded right, and Mathilde would smile and nod and say, "Oui." And then when Jodi's mum went away we asked Mathilde if what Jodi's mum had said actually DID make sense in French, and Mathilde said no.

Jodi's mum made us all this weird stuff for tea, stuff that we don't usually have at Jodi's house, and one of them was a "VEGETABLE EIFFEL TOWER". And that was probably the worst thing I've ever had at Jodi's house. But I just ate it anyway because we weren't

really there for tea; we were there on a mission.

So after tea we all sat and watched TV with Jodi's mum and waited until Jodi's mum's new boyfriend got there. Then when he got there, Jodi's mum got really excited because he had a gift for her, and it was all wrapped up in a pink bow, and I thought it looked like a box of chocolates, and it was.

Jodi said that her mum's new boyfriend always brings her chocolates, and flowers, and sometimes perfume. And he lets Jodi have all the ice-cream she wants from his ice-cream van (which is awesome!).

Sometimes Dad takes me out in his van. But my dad's a plumber, so there's no ice-cream or anything good like that in his van, just boring stuff. And sometimes it smells really bad in the van if there's been a "LOO EMERGENCY".

So anyway, Jodi waited until nobody was looking, and then she took the keys out of her mum's new boyfriend's coat. And she did it really slowly, and she held them really tight so they wouldn't jingle. And Maisie squeezed my hand so tight I made a noise, and Jodi STARED at me with her angry stare (even though it wasn't my fault!).

Then Jodi went through to the kitchen and told her mum that we were all going to Zach's. And Jodi's mum said, "All right. Make sure you phone me as soon as you get there."

Our mums always make us do that, even though we only live down the road and along a bit from each other.

So we all said bye, and then ran out of the door and down the stairs to the ice-cream van. And I was so excited I thought I was going to burst. But Maisie looked really pale, because she was scared that we were going to get put in prison for stealing an ice-cream van. But, like Jodi said, it wasn't like we were going to STEAL it; we were just going to hide Mathilde behind the box of Flakes. And then we'd put the keys back right away, and go to Zach's like we'd said.

When we got outside we saw the ice-cream van parked on the street. And Jodi said that she would go first, and open the door, and that we should stay

"OUT OF SIGHT!"

So we all hid behind a wheelie bin, and watched as Jodi ran to the van and opened the back door, and then she disappeared inside.

Mathilde clapped her hands and said, "Zee plan is going to work!" And I saw that Jodi was waving something out of the back, and that it was a Mint Aero ice-cream. And that was the sign for

"GET IN FAST!"

So we all ran, and Jodi shut the door behind us before anyone could see.

I expected it to be really dark inside the van, but it wasn't really, because it was still light outside. It smelled GREAT in there, and I couldn't stop looking at all the sweets, and the ice-creams, and I really wanted a Mint Aero or a Bounty ice-cream, but I knew if I asked Jodi that she would say no, because we were on a secret mission.

So we started moving the boxes of Flakes to make a hiding spot for Mathilde, but then we heard someone shout, **"I'VE GOT THEM!"** And we all froze. And then we heard a key turn in the lock. And we knew we were locked in. And that we must be **"THEM"**. And that we were being kidnapped!

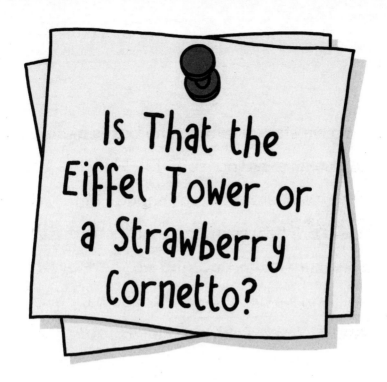

Is That the Eiffel Tower or a Strawberry Cornetto?

I was trying not to panic. But it was hard, because Maisie had fainted on me, and I was squashed up against the fridge, and I'd sat on a Twister, and it was cold and wet, and also because we were being kidnapped!

And then Mathilde whispered, "It eez my

parents! They have found out about zee secret meession!"

But then we heard someone singing! And Jodi said, "That's my mum's BOYFRIEND!"

So then I looked at Jodi. And Jodi looked at me. And we both knew what had happened. We had left the keys in the lock! And Jodi's mum's boyfriend must have been looking for his keys, and then he must have found them, and he must have just thought he'd left them in the door by mistake.

And then we heard the engine starting. And then we were moving. And we didn't know where we were going, but we knew that we were trapped.

Then Maisie woke up and we told her what was happening. And Maisie was relieved that we weren't really being kidnapped on purpose, and only by accident.

But then she said, "WAIT! We must be going to FRANCE to deliver the ice-creams!" And I realised that Maisie was right.

Mathilde said, "It eez OK. You will LOVE zee France. You can all live with ME!"

But then the ice-cream van stopped. And we heard Jodi's mum's boyfriend getting out. And we could hear voices and noises outside, but we didn't know where we were. And then we started to hear singing again, and even though it was a serious situation I wanted to laugh because Jodi's mum's boyfriend sings in a really high, shaky woman's voice, and it's funny. And then Jodi's mum's boyfriend got back in the car and we started moving again. That's when Jodi said that she could smell tuna mayonnaise, and that France was really far, and that her mum's boyfriend had probably stopped to get a sandwich. And that's when I realised that this was REALLY happening. And that we were REALLY going to France. And that my mum was going to go MAD! Because I am not even allowed to go past Jodi's house on my own, so I don't think I'm allowed to leave the country, even though Mum has not actually said that.

We were driving for ages and ages. Zach fell asleep, and so did Maisie. But me and Jodi just stayed awake. And so did Mathilde. And then we eventually stopped. And we heard Jodi's mum's boyfriend getting out. And then we heard him walking away. And then we were on our own.

Then Mathilde said, "We are in Paree! I know it!"

So we tried to look outside to see if we could see the Eiffel Tower, but it was too dark, and there was a huge Strawberry Cornetto sticker in the way.

And then Mathilde said, "You did it! Thank

you! We're are OK now, no?"

And Jodi said, "We're OK now."

But by that time Maisie was HYSTERICAL, and she started squealing, "No, Mathilde! We're not OK! We're trapped in an ice-cream van, and nobody knows where we are, and we'll probably be stuck here all night until someone eventually finds us, and by that time we will have probably all STARVED TO DEATH!"

And then we all started to get a bit worried, even Jodi, because we WERE trapped. And then Maisie started crying and said that she didn't want to be in France, and that she wanted to be in Scotland. And that she missed her mum. And that she wanted to go to her bed with the little curtains because it was late. And it WAS late, but none of us knew what time it was because none of us had watches.

And then Zach said that he thought we were going to die of STARVATION if somebody didn't find us soon. And that he didn't want his mum to have to live on her own, now that his dad had moved out for good.

And then Zach started crying even more than Maisie. And I knew that Zach probably wasn't crying because we were trapped in an ice-cream van in France, and that he was probably crying because of his dad moving out for good.

And then Mathilde said, "No more crying! We will eat ALL zee ice-cream so that we survive zee night alive!" And then she made two HUGE ice-cream cones with the swirly machine, and then she said, "I will do it special, like zee ones we get in Paree!" And then Mathilde put strawberry sauce, chocolate sauce AND banana sauce all over the cones. And then she put FIVE FLAKES in each!

Mathilde gave one to Maisie first, and then one to Zach, and then she made the same for me and Jodi. And it was BRILLIANT! And then Jodi got the giggles, because she sometimes gets the giggles if she has too many sweets and stuff.

And Jodi said, "Do you remember when we thought Mathilde was a Spy Boss on an international secret mission to steal hidden treasure?" And then she burst out laughing for ages, and strawberry sauce came out of her nose.

Then Mathilde said, "What eez a Spy Boss? You are so crazy!" And we all burst out laughing, even Maisie!

And then Jodi screamed, **"SHEPHERD'S PIE SPY!!"** And then she laughed so much she couldn't get up off the floor.

And then Mathilde said, "What eez zee shepherd's pie?" And so we told Mathilde all about the Shepherd's Pie Test, and about how shepherd's pie is DISGUSTING, and about how all the teachers put theirs in the bin.

And then Mathilde laughed too and said, "I think it tastes good, no?" And we all laughed until tears came out and our cheeks started to hurt.

Mathilde made us tell her all about our plans, and how we used to think she was a grown-up School Inspector Spy. And then she laughed for ages and ages, and she kept calling us "CRAZY" and it was hilarious. And we made sure that we ate loads and loads of ice-cream so that we didn't starve to death.

And then I was just thinking that it must be morning by now, and that's when Maisie was sick. And then Zach saw that Maisie was sick, and that made him sick too, because Zach is always sick when he sees other people being sick.

And I looked at Jodi, and she was still giggling, but she looked like she was going to be sick too, and I knew it was from all the ice-cream and all the laughing.

Then we heard a noise outside. And we all screamed, **"HELP! WE'RE TRAPPED INSIDE THE ICE-CREAM VAN!"** And then the doors flew open and we saw two policemen standing there.

And Zach shouted, "WE'RE SAVED!"

And Mathilde started speaking to them in really fast French, but they looked confused, and that's when I realised that they weren't French police officers, and that they were Scottish police officers, and that WE WERE STILL IN SCOTLAND!

And then we saw that we were right outside Jodi's house again! And we were shocked, because we thought we were definitely in Paris!

And then I saw Jodi's mum, and she was crying, and so was her new boyfriend. And I thought that he was probably crying because he felt bad for being the one who had locked us in. And then I saw Zach's mum and she looked like she had been crying too. And then I saw my mum, and she looked mad.

And then Mathilde said, "*Maman!*" and I saw that Mathilde's mum and dad were there too.

And then someone in the crowd screamed, **"ANGEL WINGS!"** And it was Maisie's mum. But then Maisie's

mum took one look at the state of Maisie, covered in all the colourful ice-cream sick, and she fainted. And she had to be taken away on a stretcher.

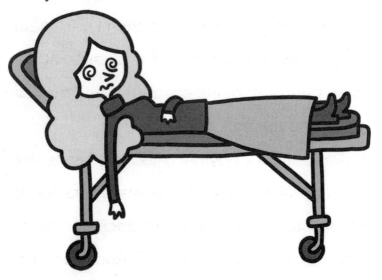

Mum and Dad gave me a big hug and then they said I was in **BIG TROUBLE**. And then Mum gave me another hug, and loads of kisses.

Everyone kept asking if we were OK, and I said that we were but that we felt a bit sick from all the ice-cream. And then I told them about how we had to eat it all so that we didn't starve to death overnight. And they all started laughing.

Jodi's mum's boyfriend looked inside the van and said, "Wow. You've made a fair dent in my stock anyway! No chance of any of you starving any time soon!" And then they all laughed again, even though it wasn't funny, and they were probably just laughing because they were in shock.

And then Jodi asked the police officer why it had taken him so long to EVENTUALLY find us. And she explained about how if SHE had been the one looking for us, she was sure she would have found us at least ten hours before they did.

And then the police officer looked a bit annoyed. And then he said that they had found the fake order and the orange squash bottle full of 5p's behind the wheelie bin. And that's when we remembered we'd forgotten to bring them with us. And that we had forgotten to put it in the front of the van so Jodi's mum's boyfriend would find it.

And then the police officer told us that it was only 7p.m. and that he doubted Jodi would have been able to do a quicker job than he had, because we'd only been missing for an hour and a half. And then Jodi said that she didn't believe him about it only being 7p.m., and neither did I. But then he sighed and showed us his watch, and then we believed him. And then we all went home.

Crazy New Friends

On Monday we told Mathilde that we were sorry the plan didn't work. And then I said that maybe we could think of a new plan.

But Mathilde said that she didn't want to do a new plan, because she said she wasn't homesick any more, and that she liked it here now. And then she asked if we could go to The Den, so we did.

Then at lunchtime Mathilde ate all our shepherd's pie, and gave us her packed lunch. And that was brilliant because Mathilde's dad had made her LOADS of peanut butter and jelly sandwiches and three packets of these little chocolates we'd never had before, and they were THE BEST!

I'm really glad Mathilde is our friend now. But I'm a bit sad too, because Mathilde's going back to live in France next month, because she says her mum and dad are HOMESICK! And it's funny because Mathilde doesn't even WANT to leave our school now, because she says she'll miss her "CRAZY NEW FRIENDS" (that's us!). And that she'll also miss The Den, and Miss Jones, and the ice-cream van, and all the shepherd's pie! So we said we'd make sure we'd send her all of our shepherd's pie. And Mathilde's going to send us more of the little chocolates, because they're brilliant, and you don't get them in the shops here.

Mathilde's mum said that we could all come and visit Mathilde in France whenever we want. So I asked Mum, but Mum said, "Isabella! There is **NO WAY** I am letting you go **ANYWHERE** any time soon!"

But that's probably just because she's still upset about when we went missing in the ice-cream van. So I'll wait and ask her again tomorrow.

Ode to Andy

As I hold this book
And lay down my bouquet,
These words are for you
On our wedding day.

I love you like foxes,
I love you like ducks,
I love you more than Khan's
Chips, cheese and Doner Deluxe.

So let all cats rejoice and poodles
  prance,
Pugs delight and sausage dogs dance,
For today you become my husband
And I your lucky wife.
And I promise to keep you laughing
For the rest of your natural life.